Little Red Riding Hood

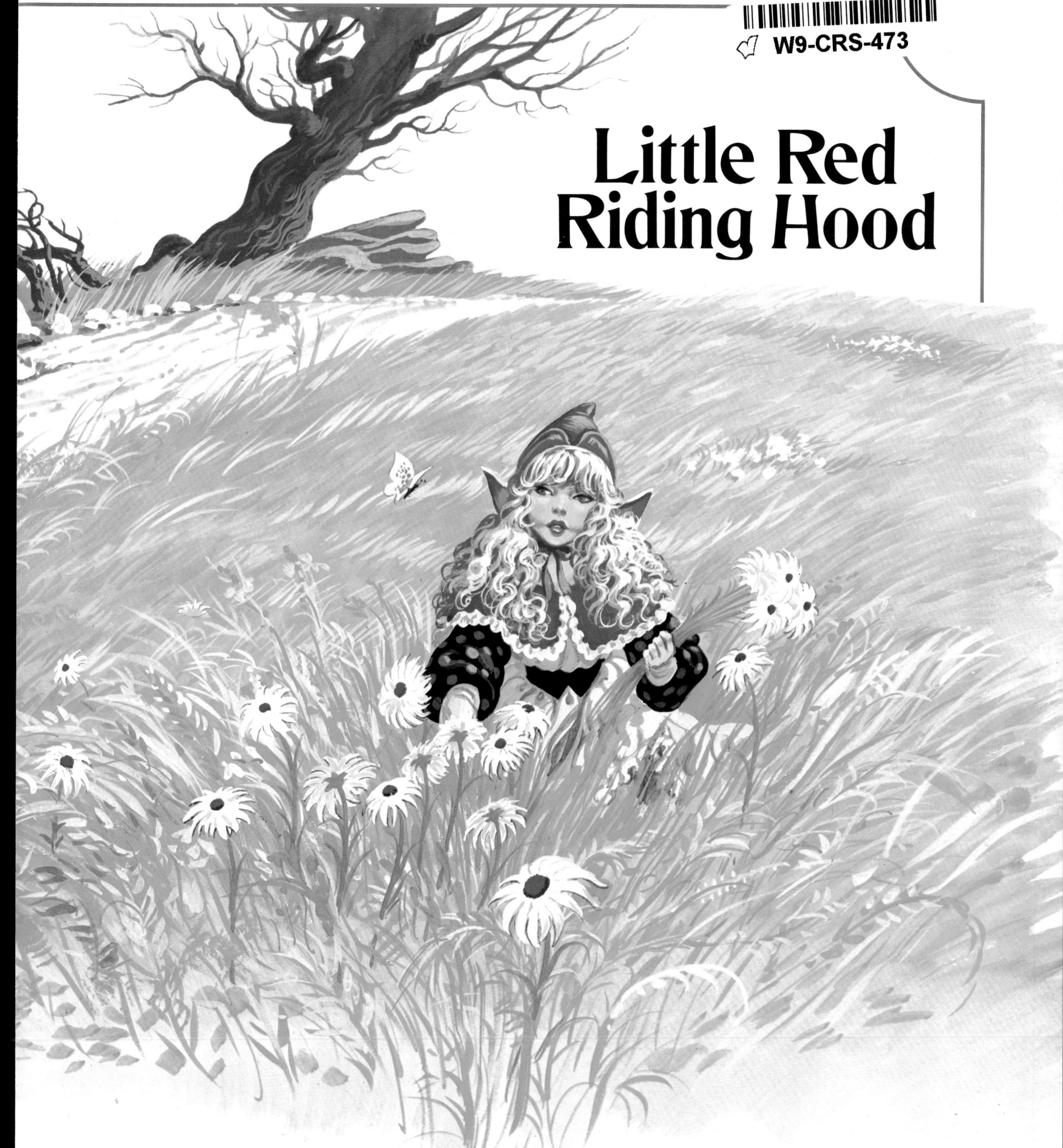

GALLERY BOOKS
An Imprint of W. H. Smith Publishers Inc
112 Madison Avenue
New York City 10016

Once upon a time there was a little girl who was as sweet and good as she could be. She and her mother lived in a small house at the edge of a forest.

The little girl often wore a pretty red cape and hood that her grandmother had made for her. She looked so gay and charming in it, that everyone called her Little Red Riding Hood.

One sunny morning, Little Red Riding Hood was playing outside when her mother called to her.

"Go, my child, and visit your grandmother," she said. "I hear she has been ill. Take her this basket of fresh bread and cheese and this small pot of hot tea."

She handed the basket to Little Red Riding Hood and reminded her, "Go straight to Grandmother's house. Do not talk to strangers or stop to play along the way."

Little Red Riding Hood waved goodbye to her mother and started down the path to her grandmother's house, which was on the other side of the woods.

She had walked this way many times before with her mother. But this was the first time she had gone by herself.

As she skipped along the path through the forest, she saw small animals hiding in the underbrush. Squirrels and chipmunks were searching for berries to eat. A family of rabbits, nestled under a bed of ferns, crept out quietly to peek at her as she passed by. From a nearby tree, an owl called, "Whoooo. Whoooo. Whoooo."

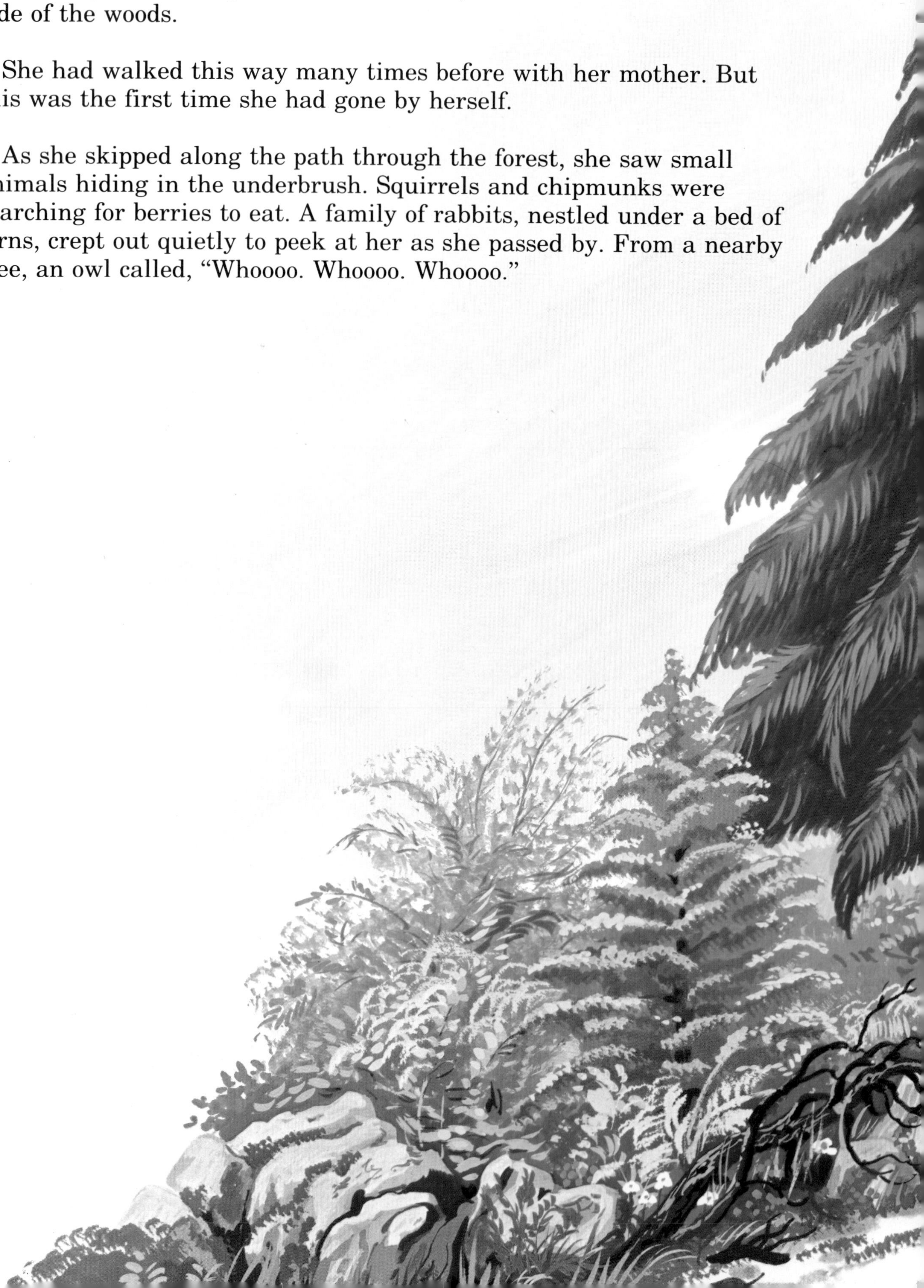

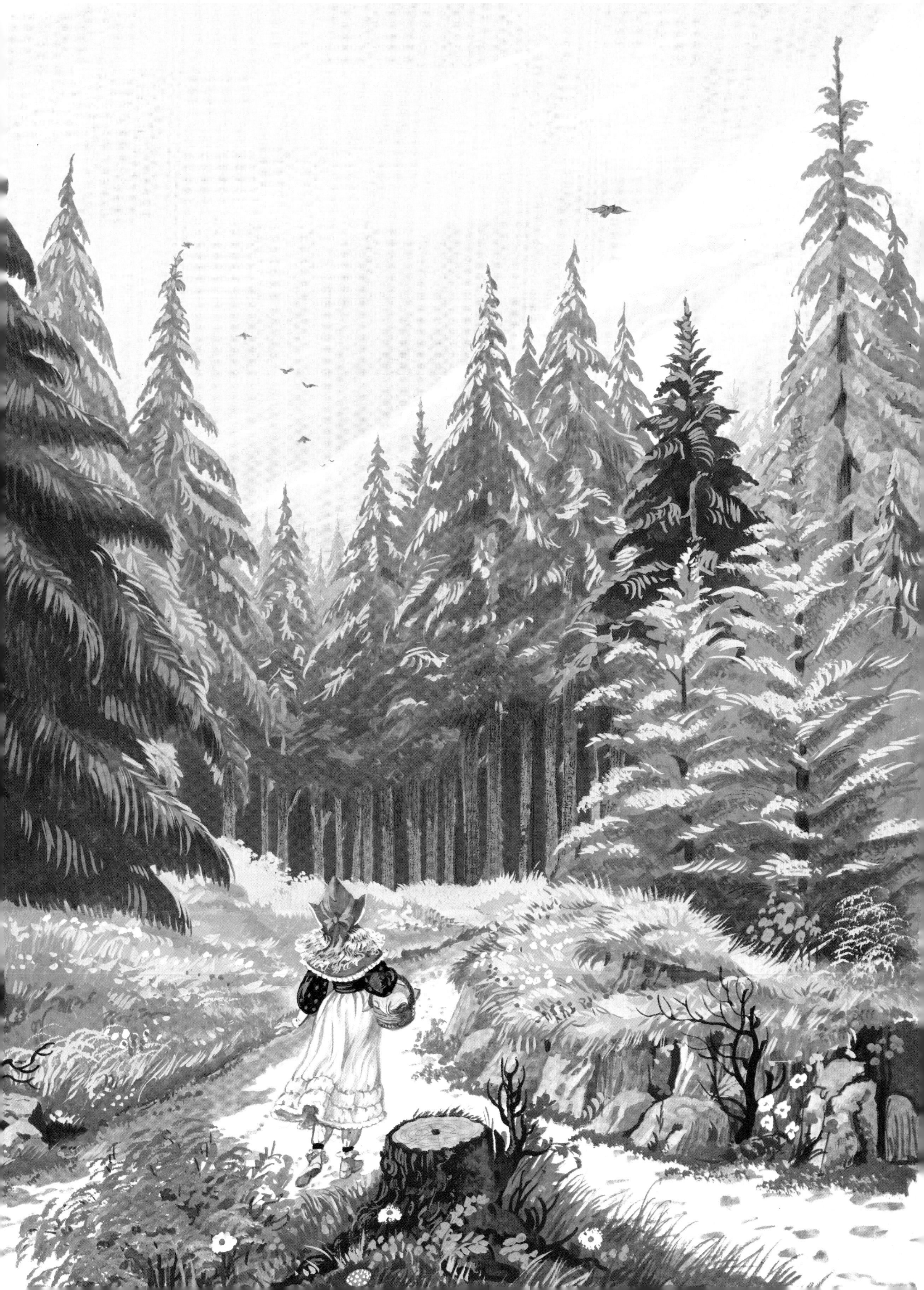

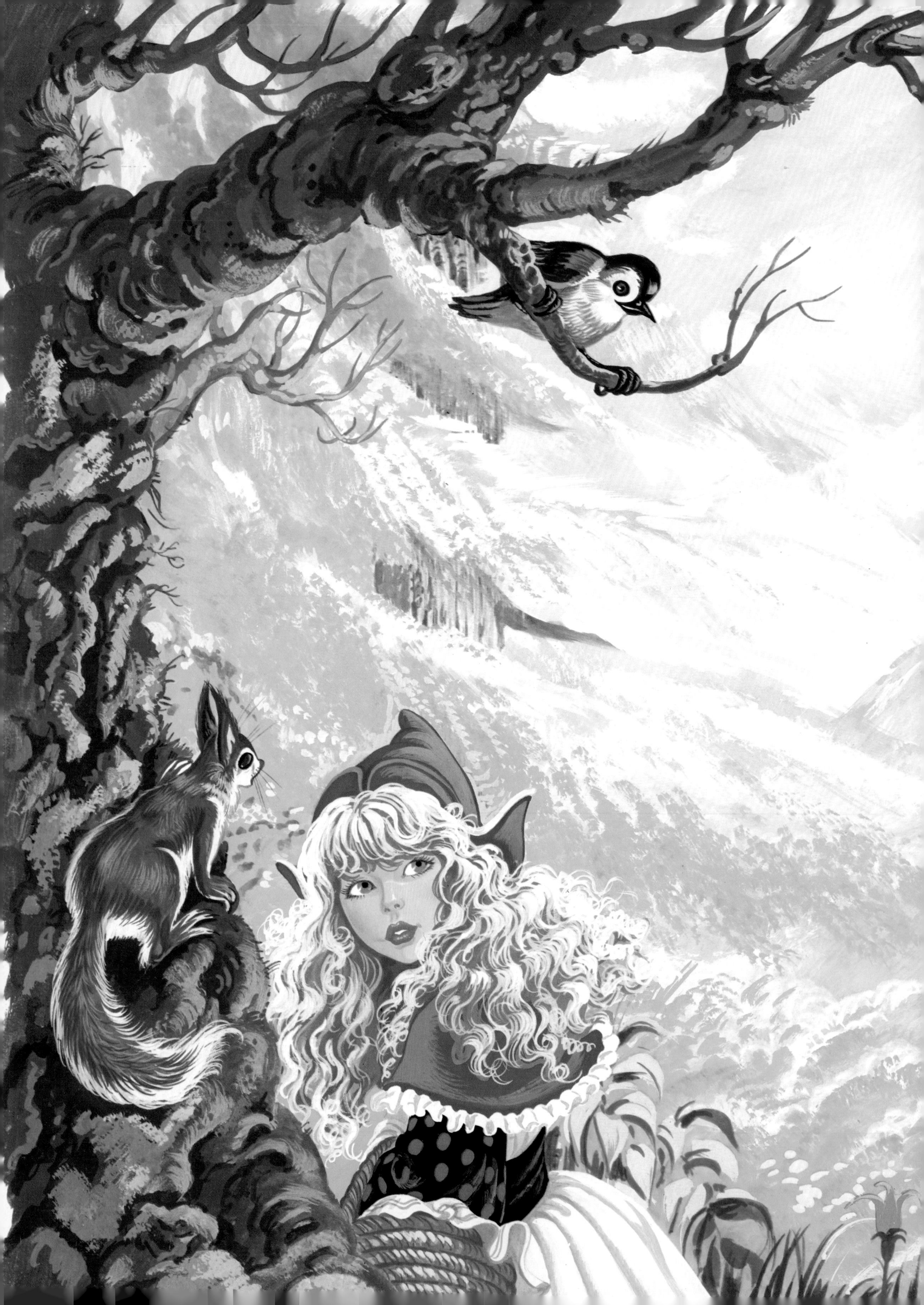

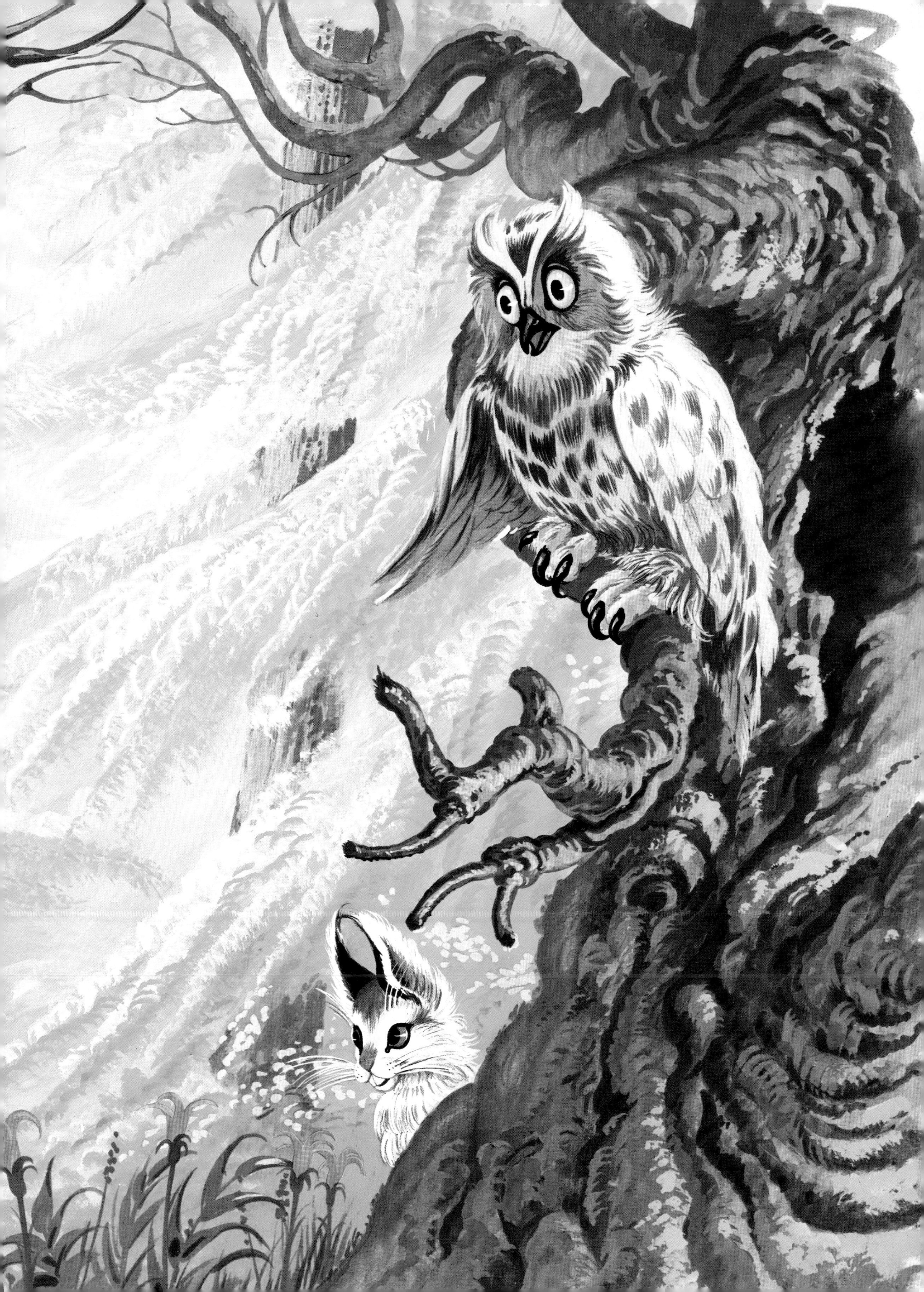

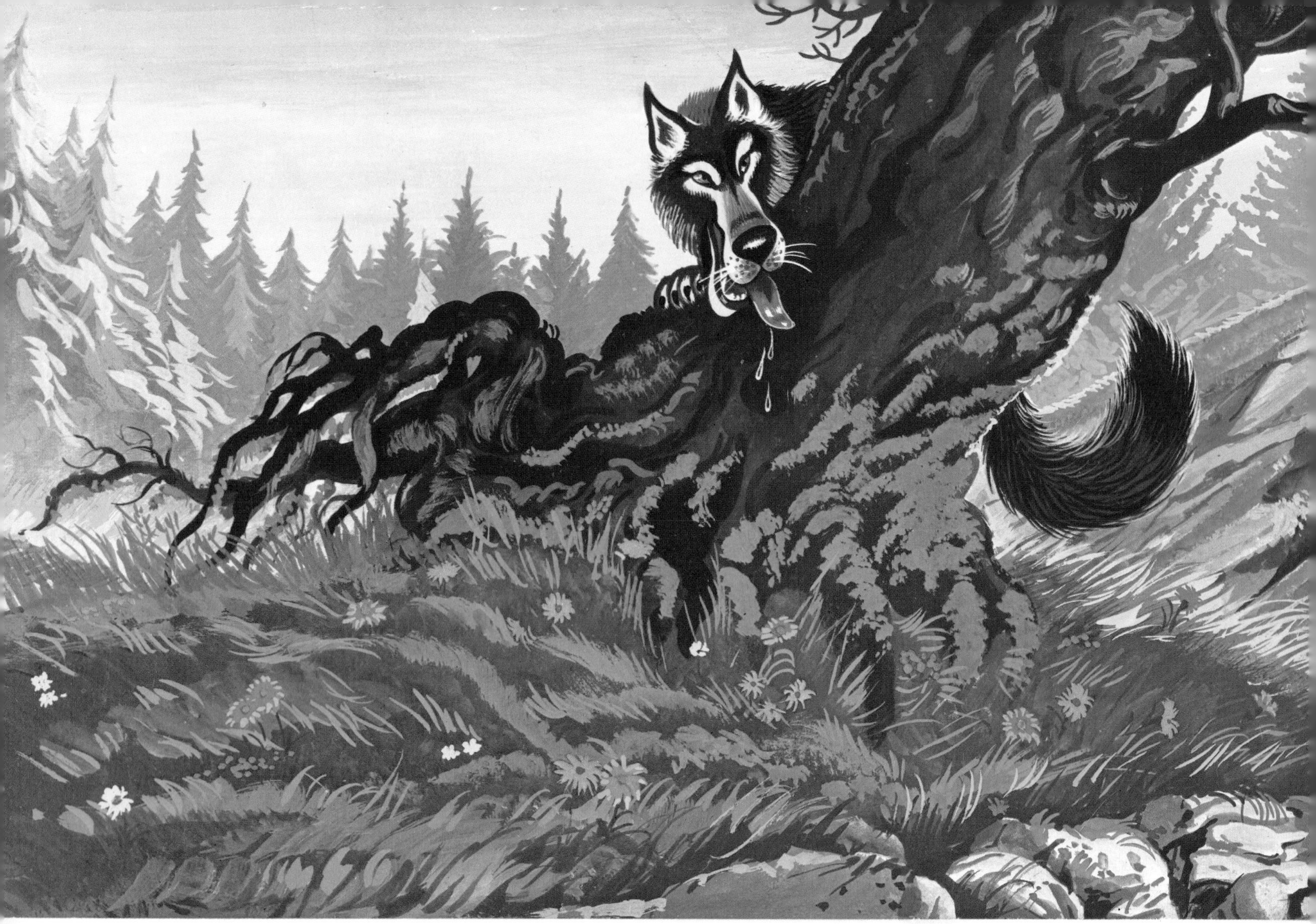

Little Red Riding Hood hurried along the path. Soon she came to a clearing in the forest. There she was surprised to see a wolf standing behind a tree.

The wolf was very hungry. He had not eaten a bite in four days. His mouth watered as he looked at Little Red Riding Hood and her basket of goodies. He wanted to eat her up right then and there. But some woodcutters were nearby, and he did not dare.

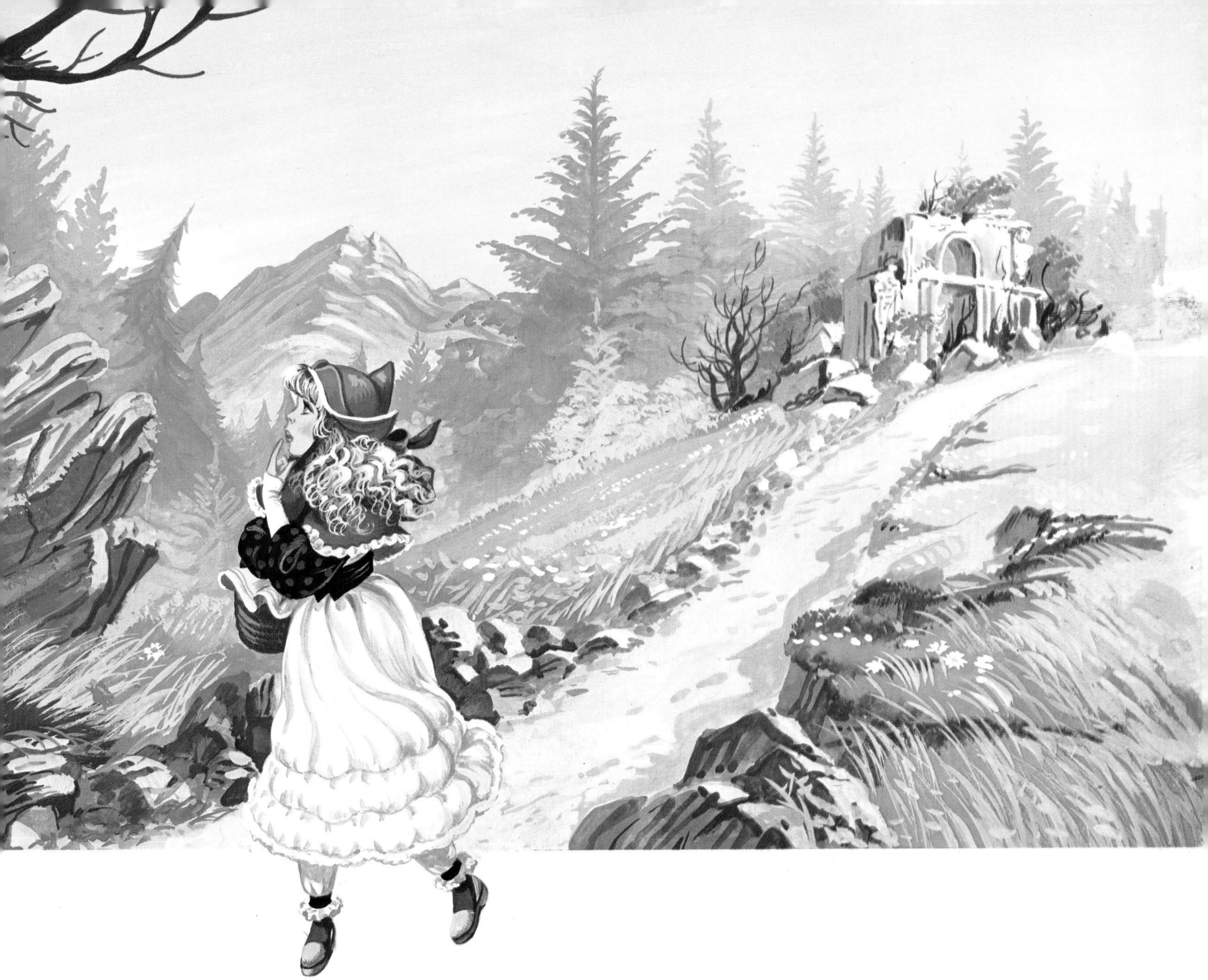

"Good morning, little girl," the wolf said to Little Red Riding Hood. "Where are you going on this fine day?"

Little Red Riding Hood did not know that it was dangerous to talk to a wolf. She answered, "I am going to visit my grandmother. She is sick, and I am taking her this basket of food."

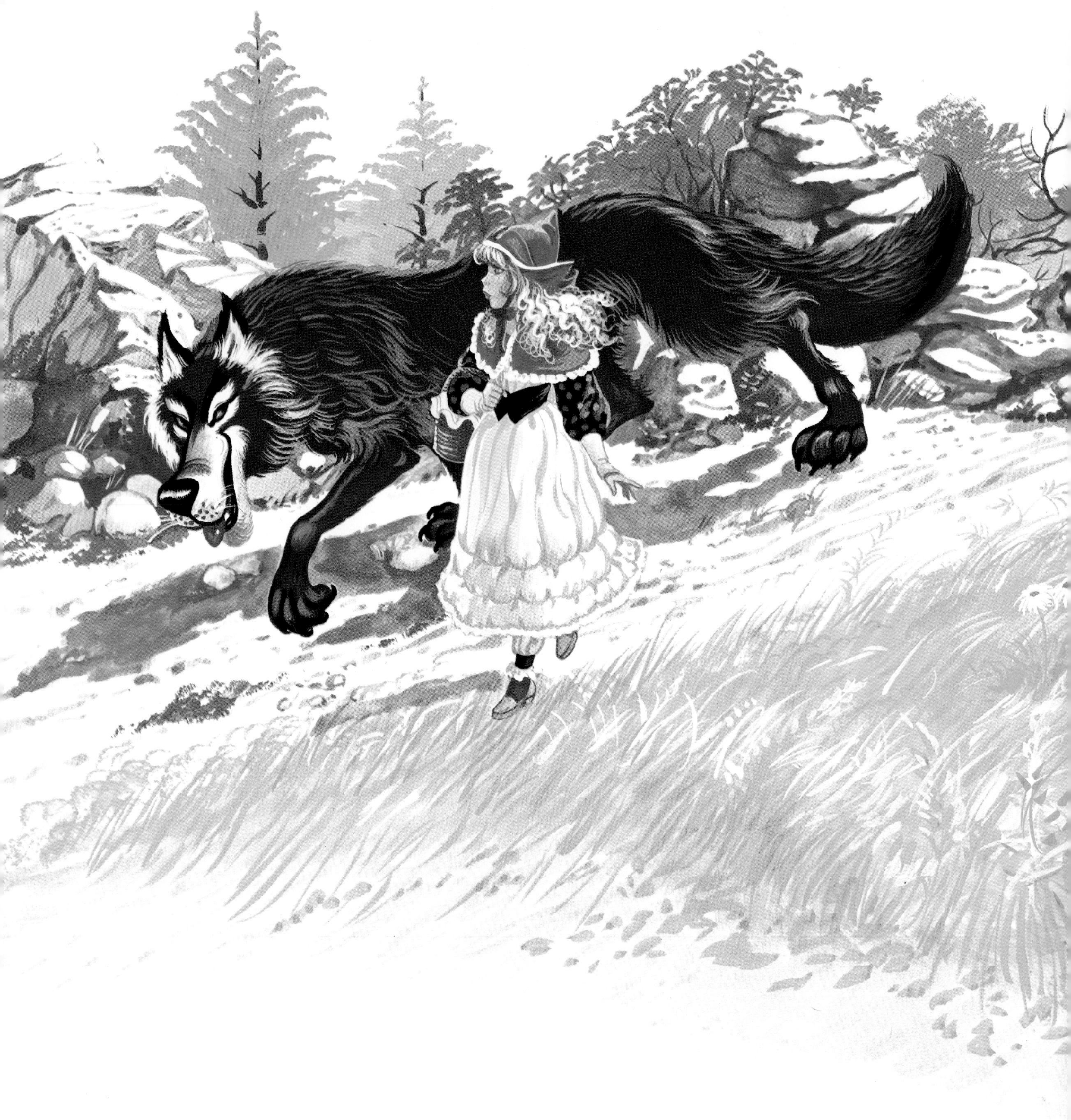

“Do you have far to go?” asked the wolf.

“Oh, yes,” said Little Red Riding Hood. “My grandmother lives on the other side of the forest. Her house is the one with a red roof and a white stone wall around the yard.”

The wolf grinned and nodded his head. He started walking down the path.

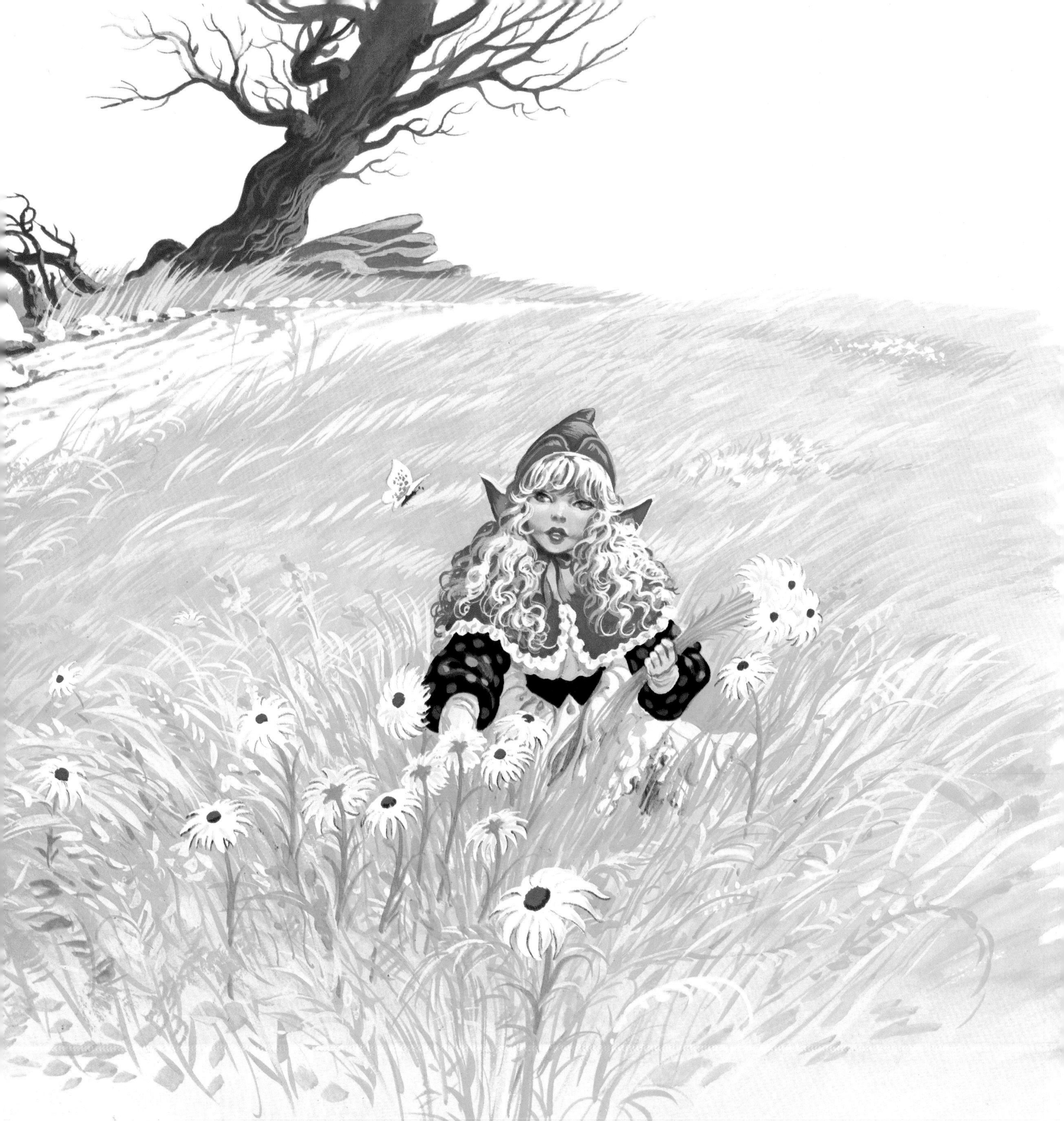

"I must be on my way," he said. "Good day to you, my dear."

"Good day," said Little Red Riding Hood.

She looked around and spied a meadow of white daisies.

"Oh, what lovely flowers," she cried. "I will pick some to take to Grandmother."

The wolf ran through the forest as fast as he could go. He knew a shorter way to the grandmother's house.

"I must get there before the little girl does," he thought.

He licked his lips as he planned what he would do next.

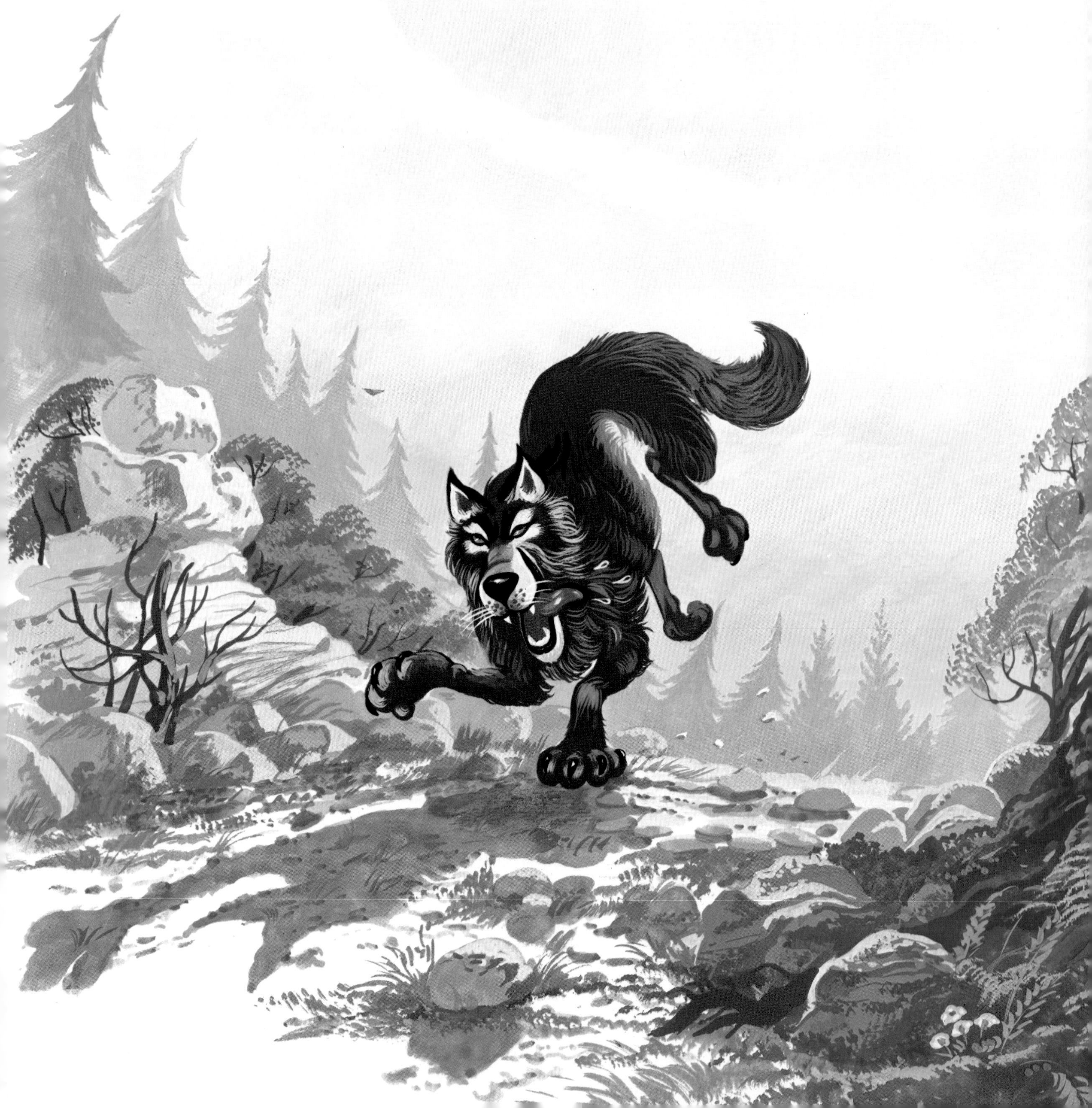

Little Red Riding Hood gathered a pretty bouquet of daisies for her grandmother.

"These flowers will surely cheer her up," she thought.

She did not know that the wolf was going to her grandmother's house. With her basket of goodies on one arm and her flowers in the other, Little Red Riding Hood continued her walk down the path.

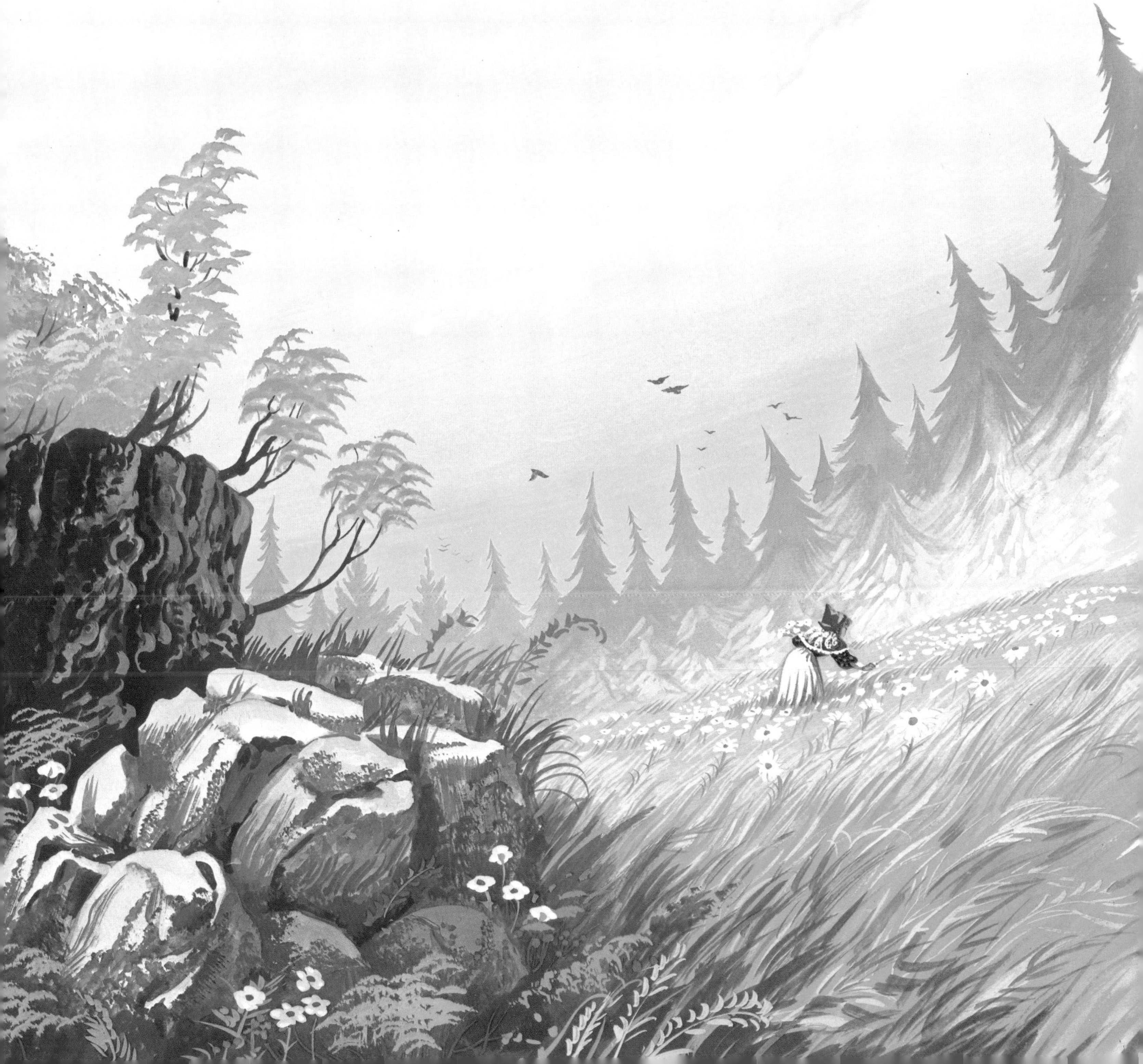

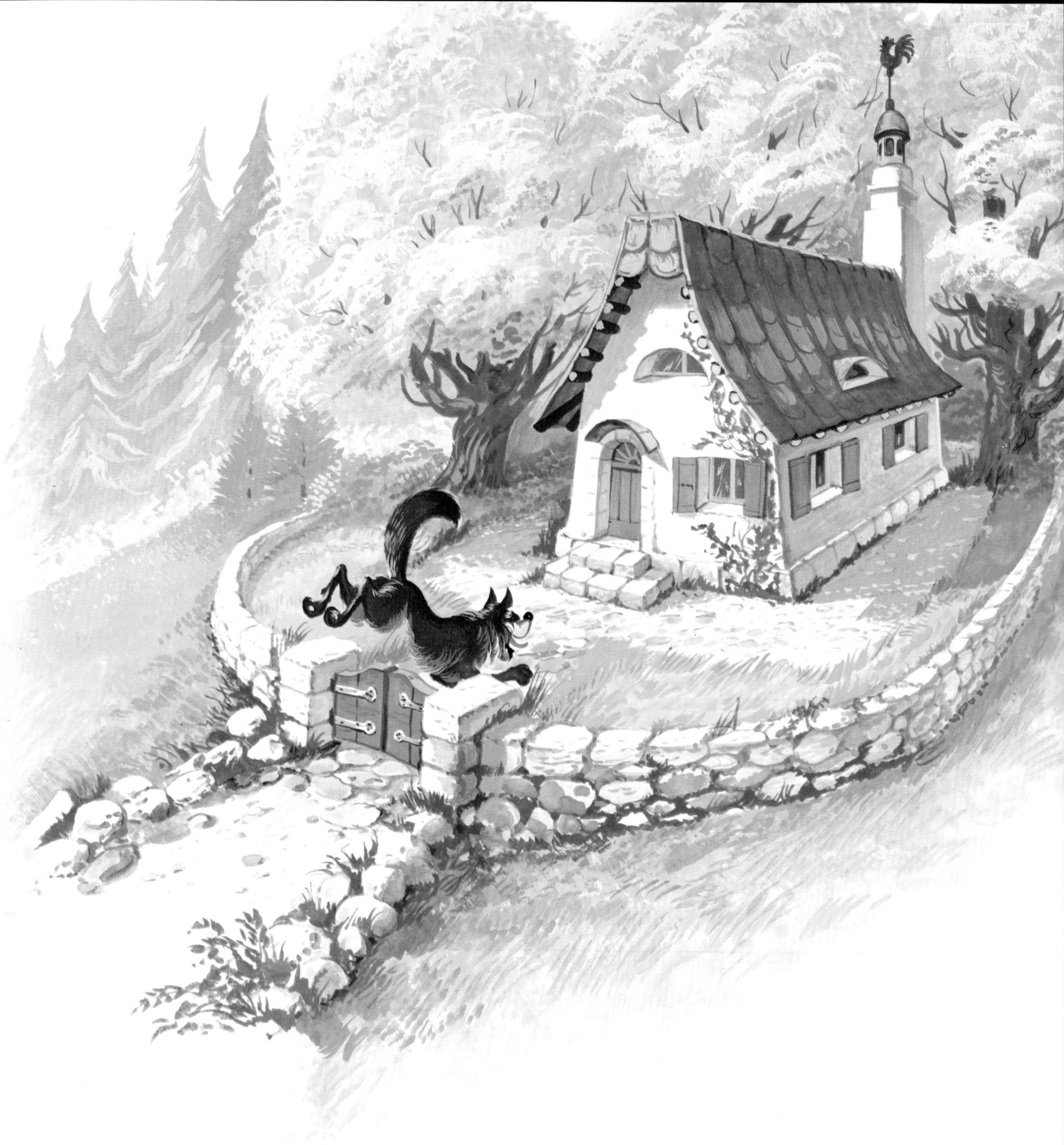

In a very short time, the wolf arrived at the grandmother's house. He knocked gently at her door.

"Who is there?" the grandmother called out. She was not feeling well and was resting in her bed.

"It is your granddaughter," said the wolf in a soft high voice.

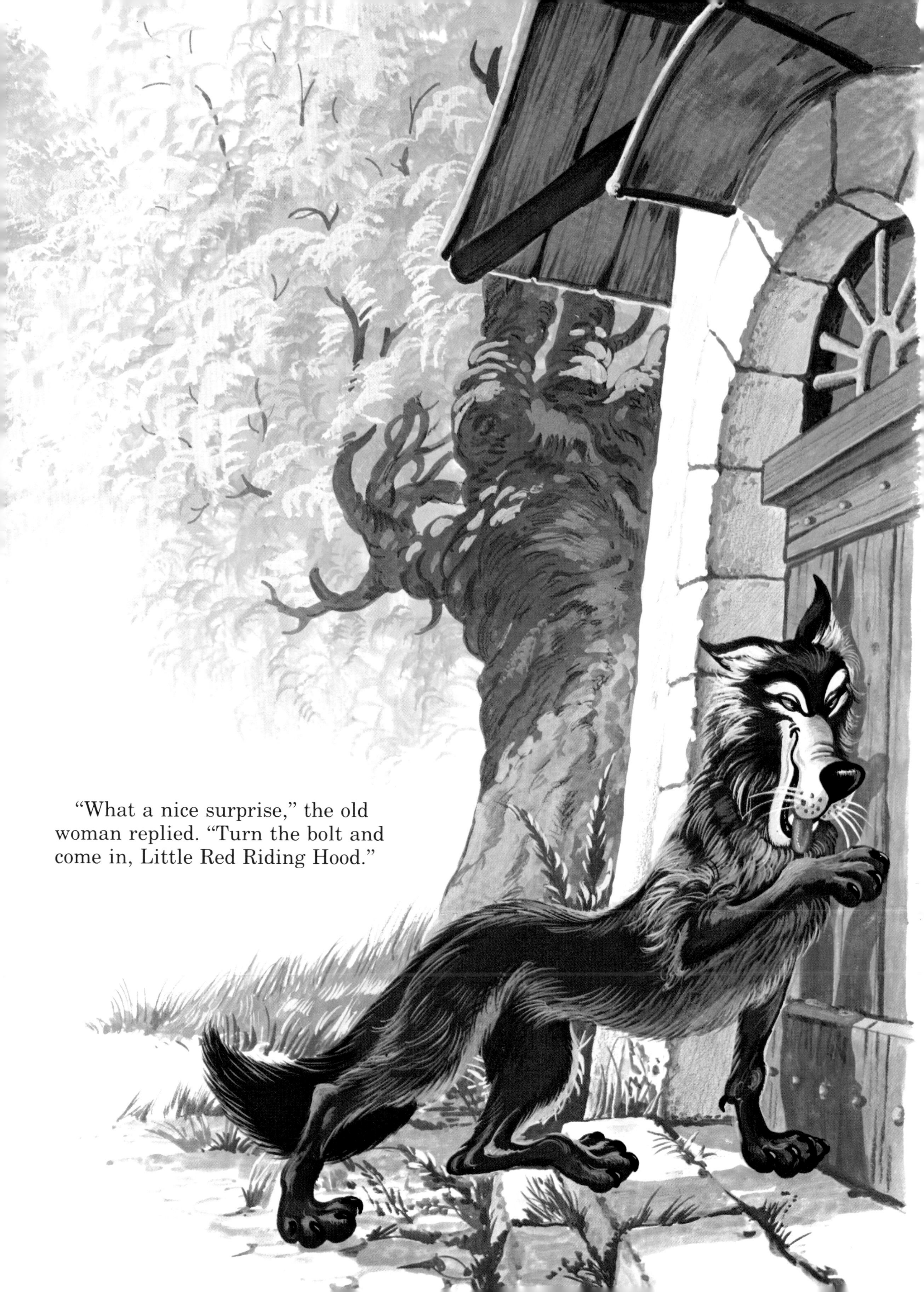

"What a nice surprise," the old woman replied. "Turn the bolt and come in, Little Red Riding Hood."

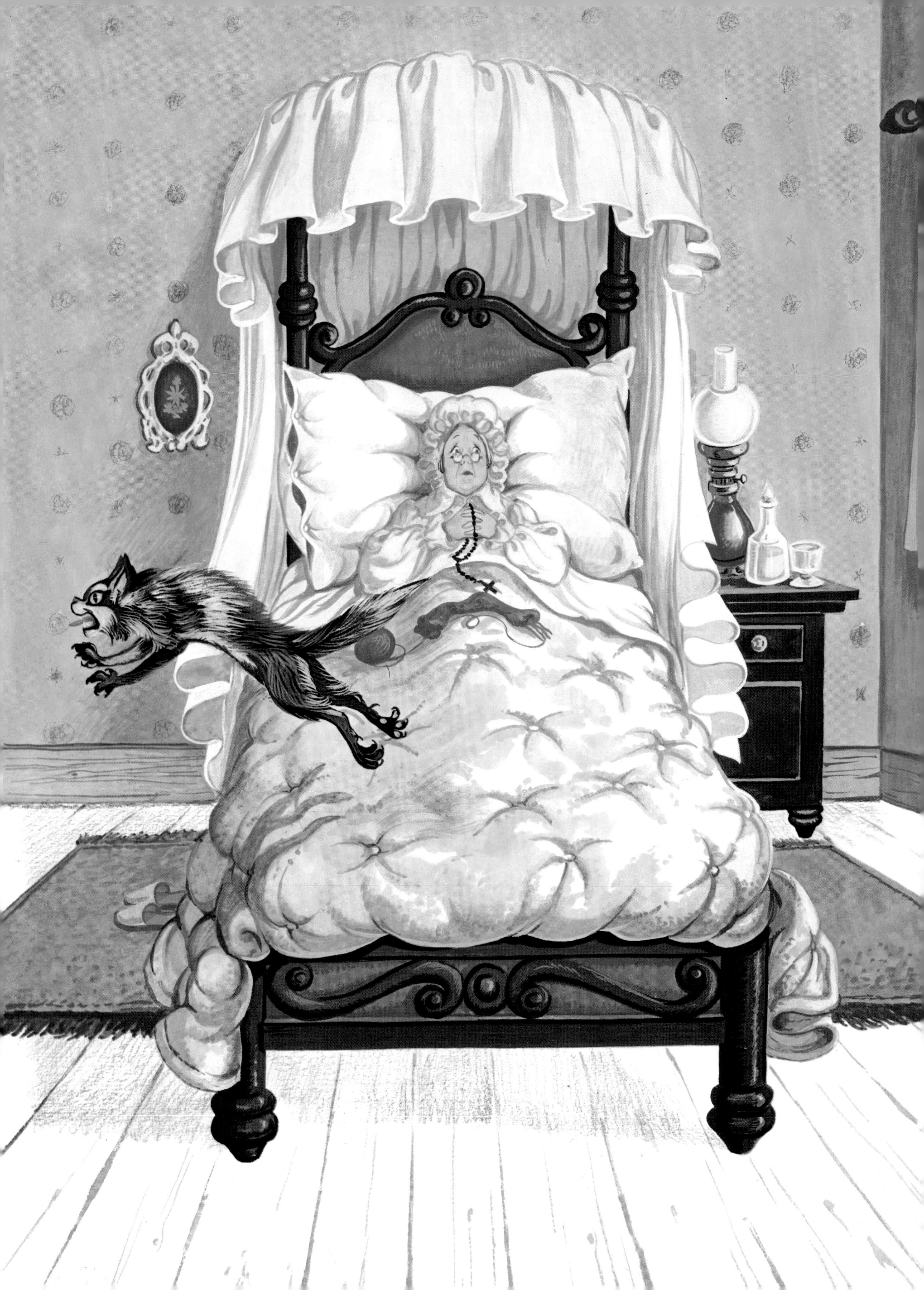

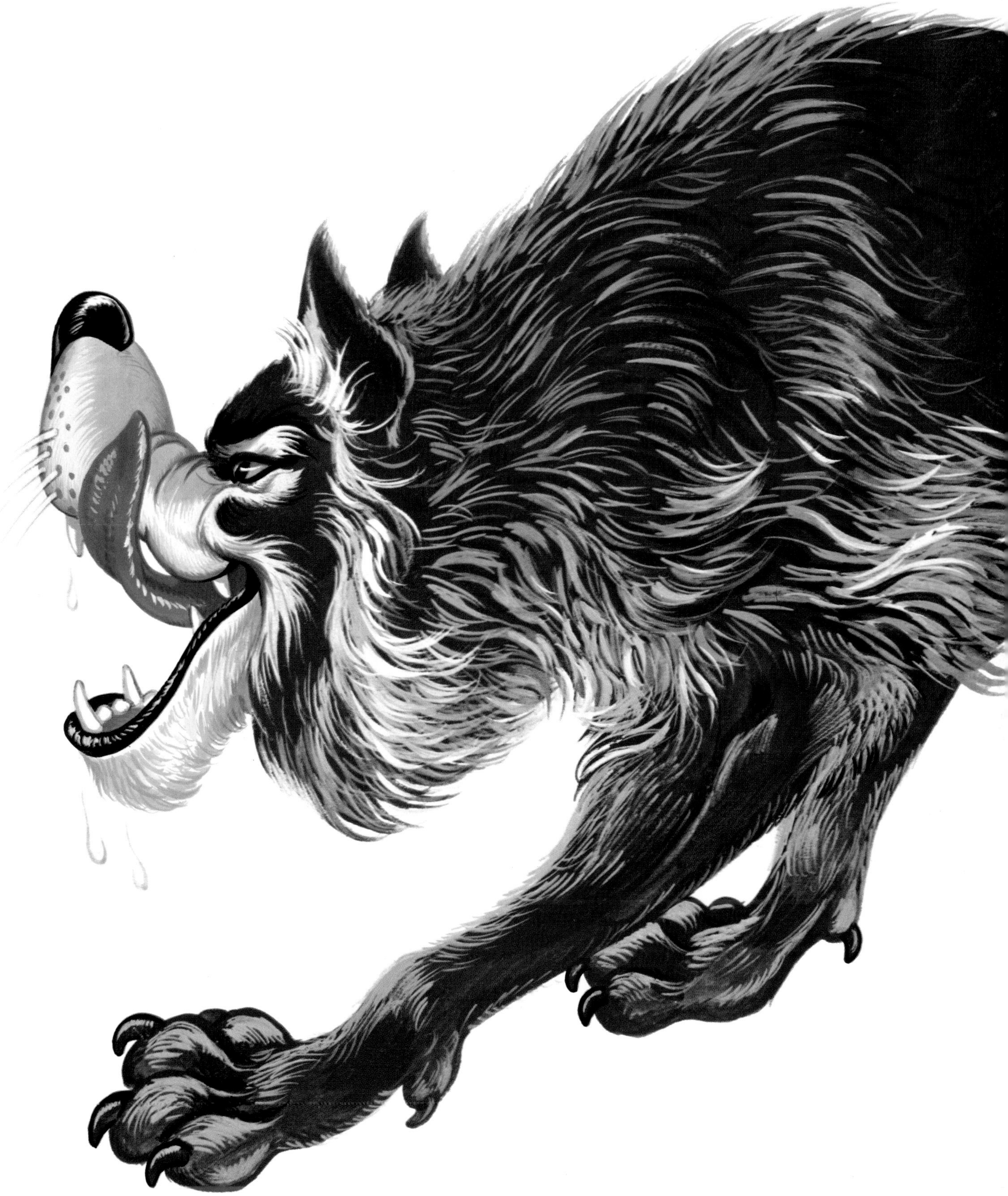

With a snarl, the wolf burst in the door. He jumped upon the poor grandmother and swallowed her in one big gulp.

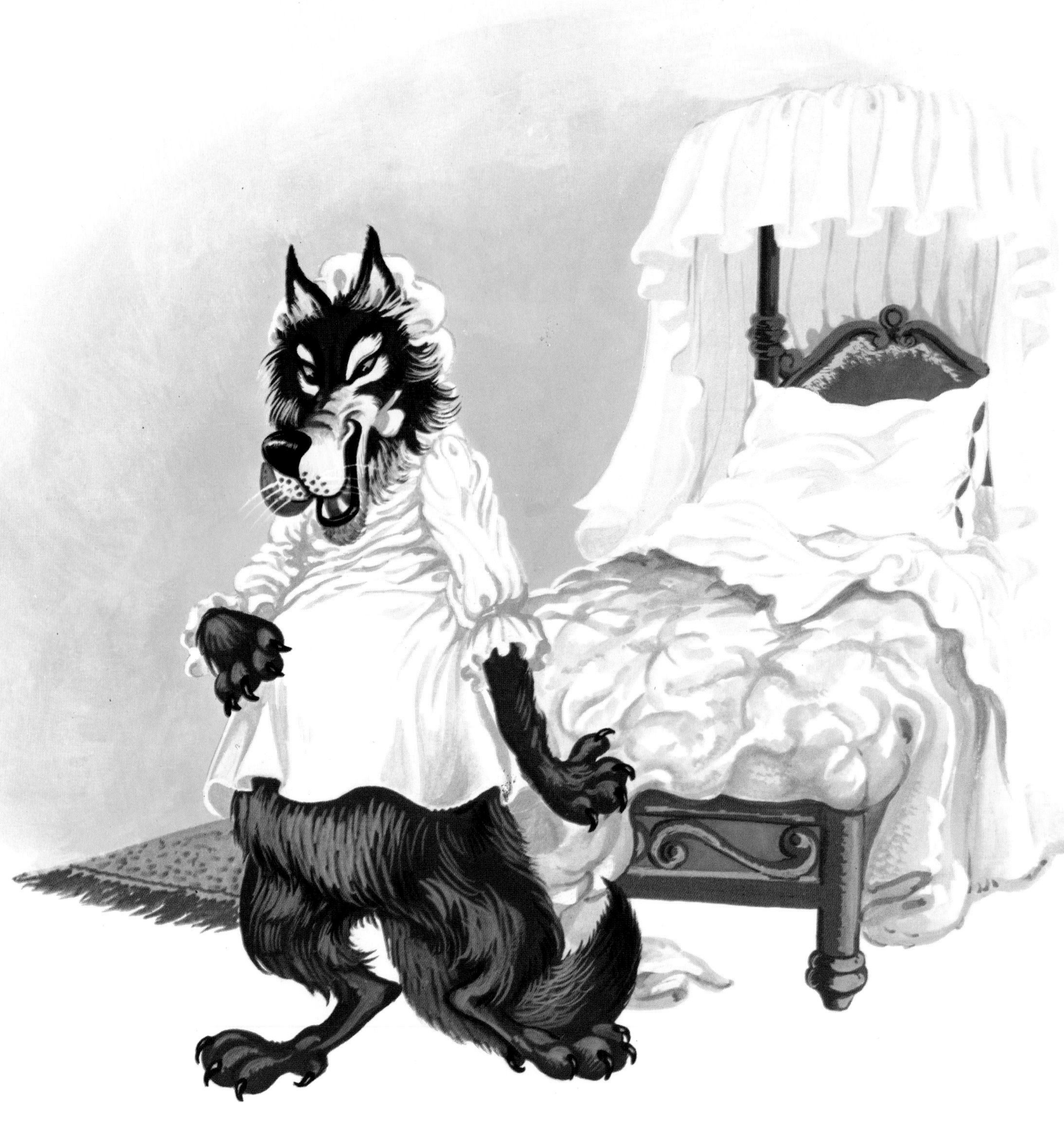

Then he put on the old woman's nightgown and cap. The nightgown did not fit very well over his full stomach. But he knew that Little Red Riding Hood would be coming soon.

The wolf closed the door to the house. Then he climbed into the grandmother's bed to wait for Little Red Riding Hood.

"Ah, yes," he thought, "she will be a very tasty morsel indeed." He licked his lips in anticipation.

By and by, Little Red Riding Hood arrived at her grandmother's house. She knocked at the door.

"Who is there?" the wolf called out in a hoarse, quavery voice.

"It is I, Little Red Riding Hood," the little girl replied. "I have brought you some fresh bread and cheese which Mother has made for you."

"Turn the bolt and come in, my dear," the wolf replied, in as soft a voice as he could manage.

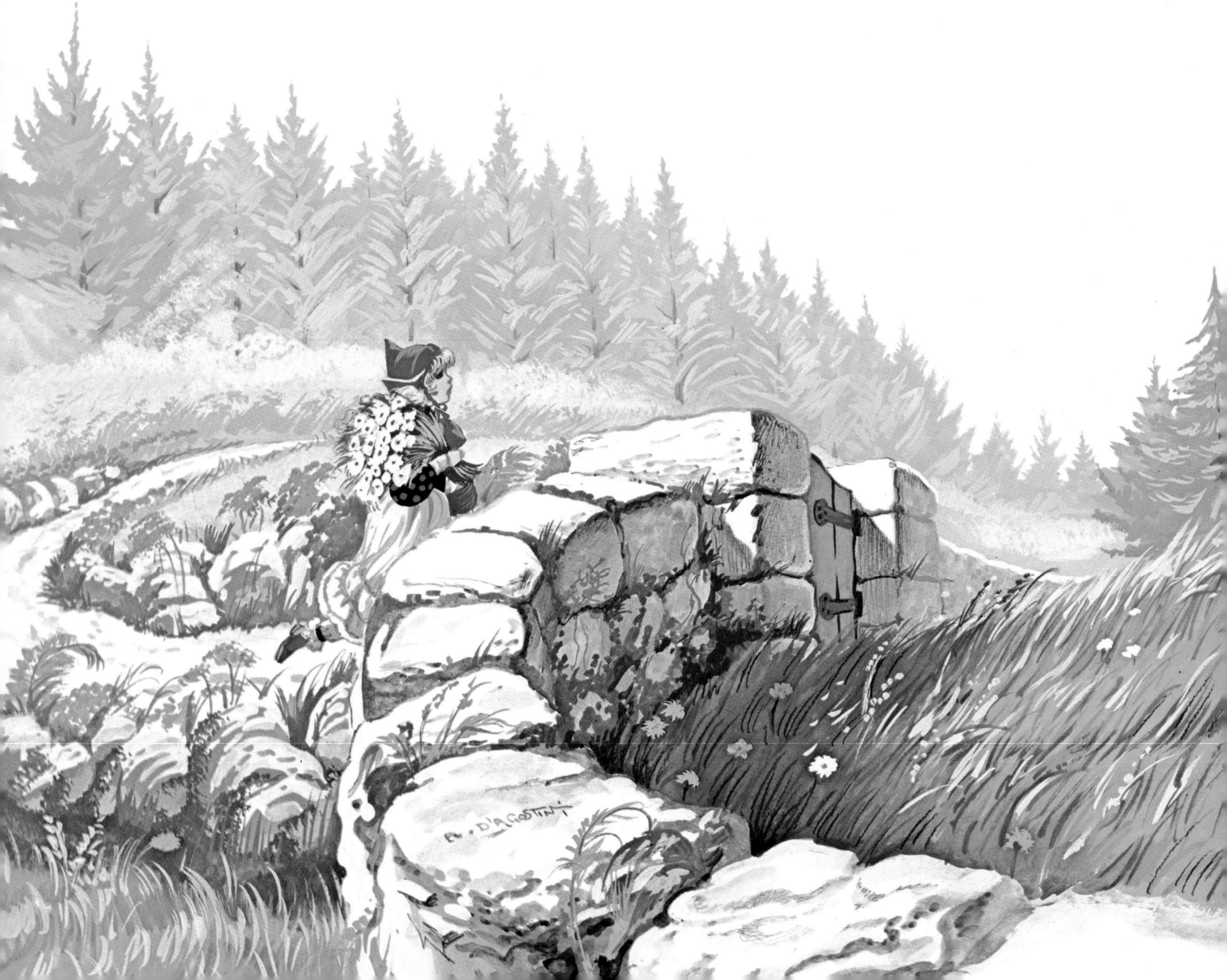

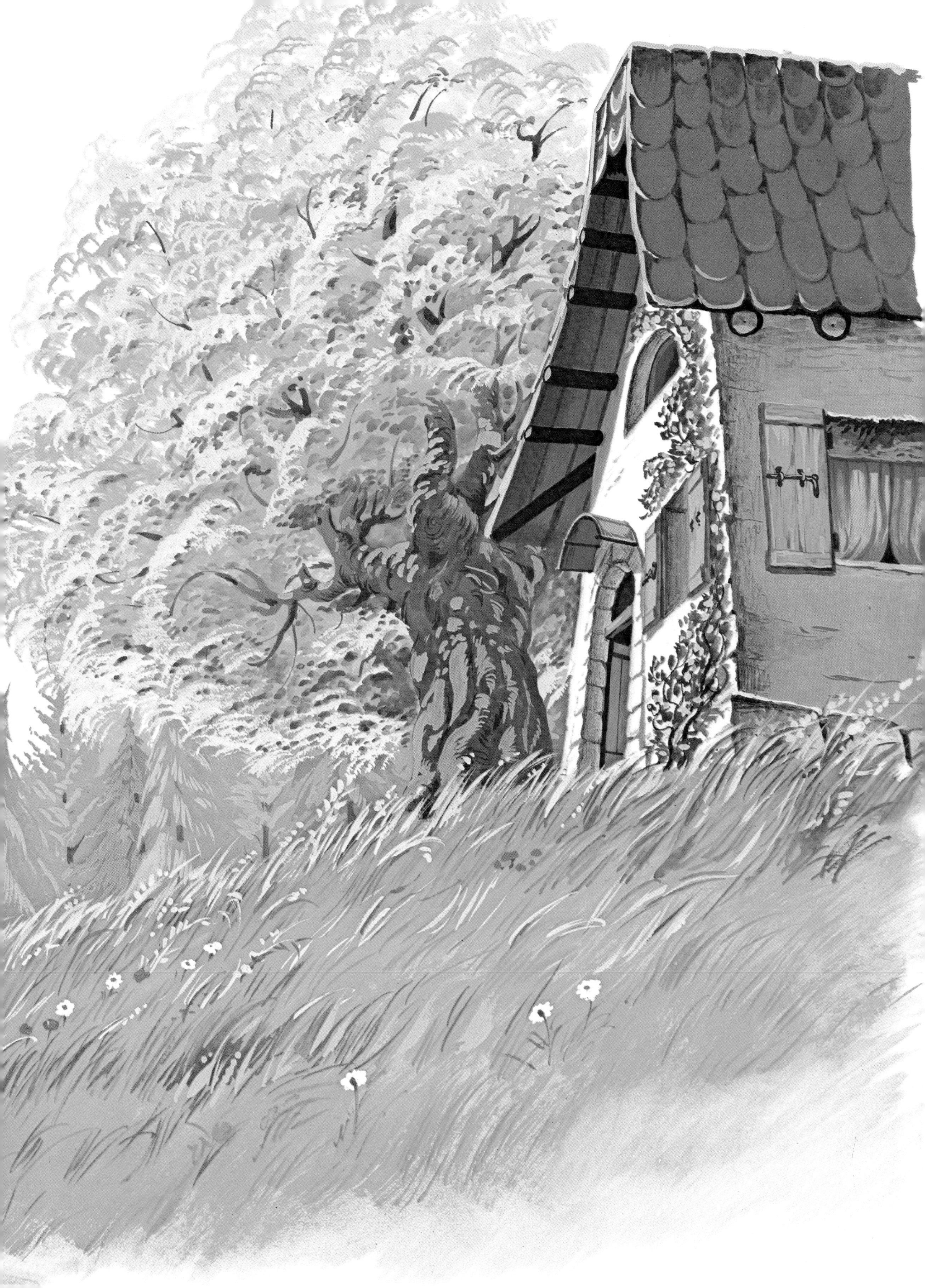

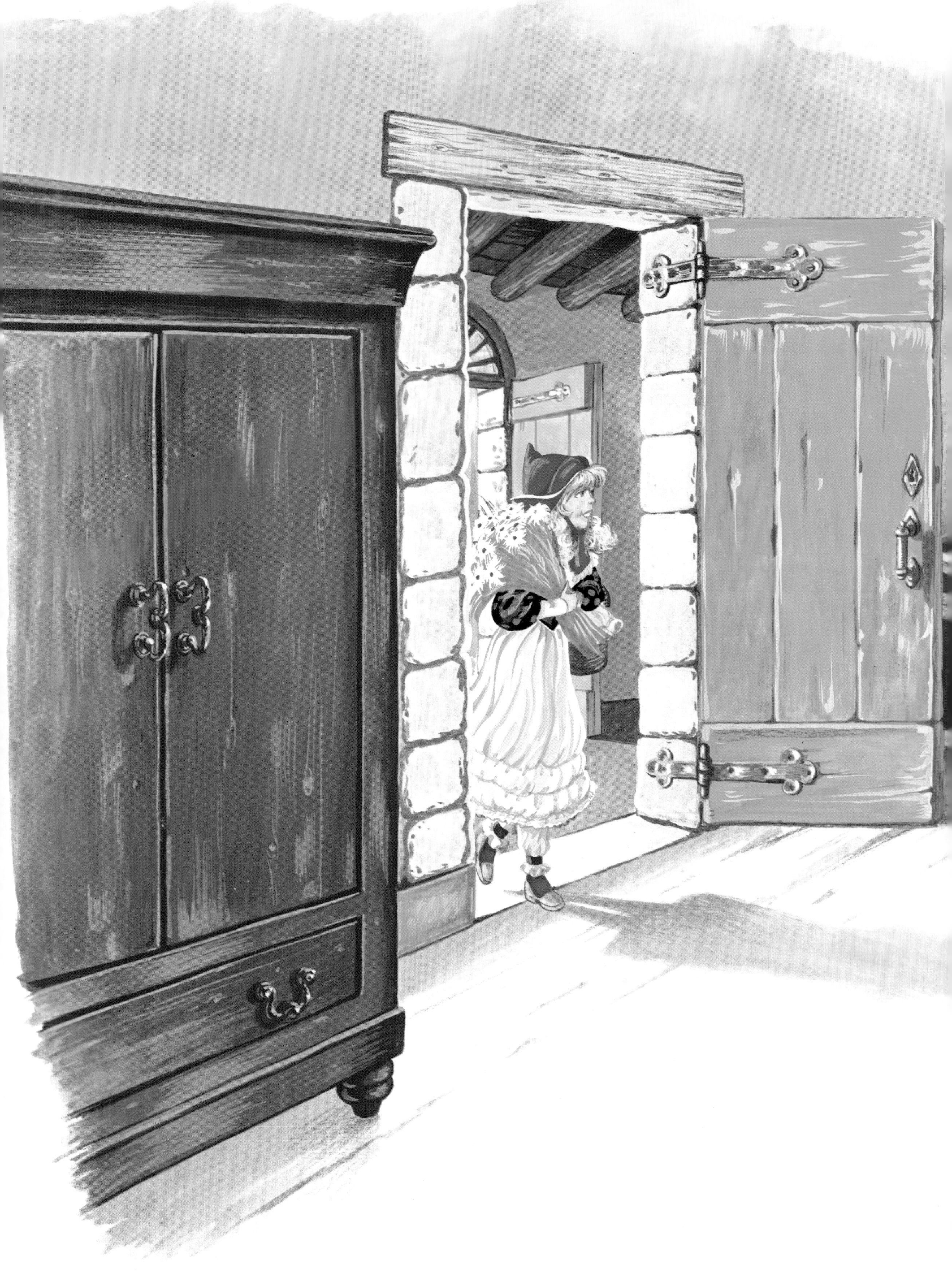

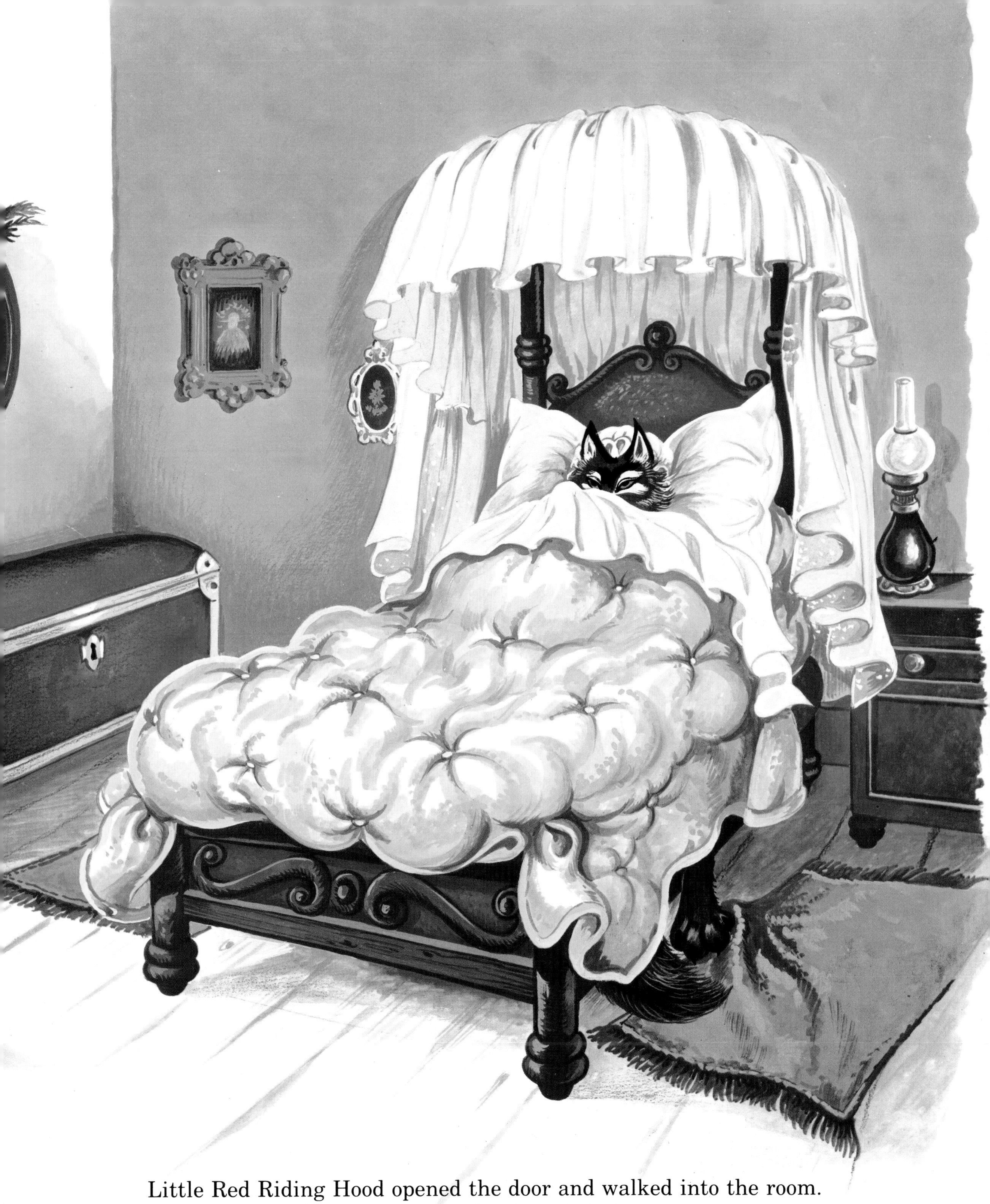

Little Red Riding Hood opened the door and walked into the room. She was surprised to see her grandmother in bed.

The wolf tried to hide himself under the sheets and blankets on the bed.

"Put the basket of food on the trunk," he said to her, "and come over here next to me."

Little Red Riding Hood did as she was told and stood beside the bed. She thought that her grandmother looked very strange in her nightgown and cap.

"Oh, Grandmother, what big eyes you have," she said.

"The better to see you with, my dear," answered the wolf.

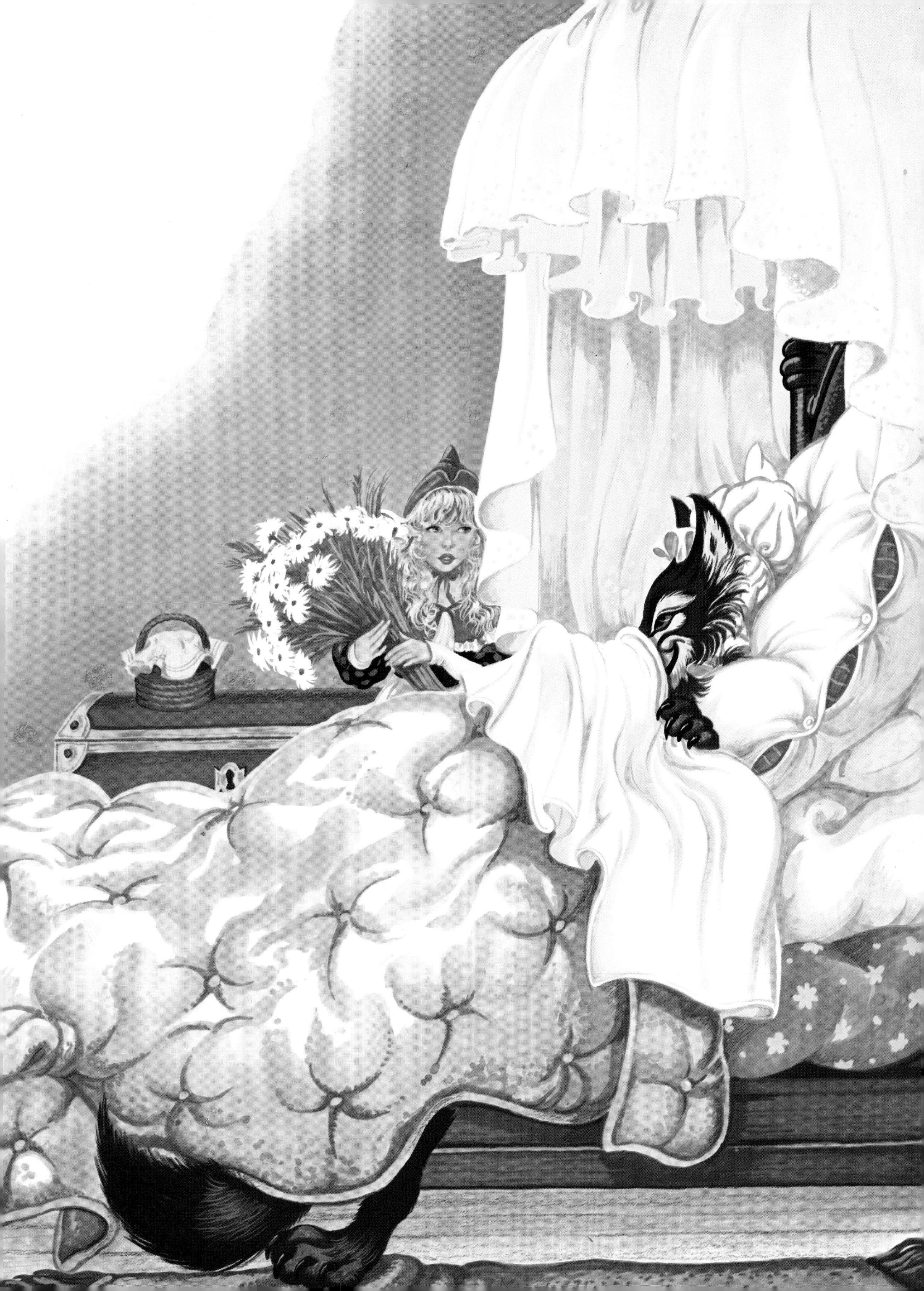

"Oh, Grandmother, what big ears you have," Little Red Riding Hood said.

"The better to hear you with, my dear," said the wolf.

"And, Grandmother, what big teeth you have," the little girl said.

"The better to eat you with, my dear," growled the wolf. He jumped out of bed and ran after her.

Little Red Riding Hood screamed for help. But the wolf leaped upon her and gobbled her up in one gulp. Then, feeling very full indeed, he lay back down on the bed.

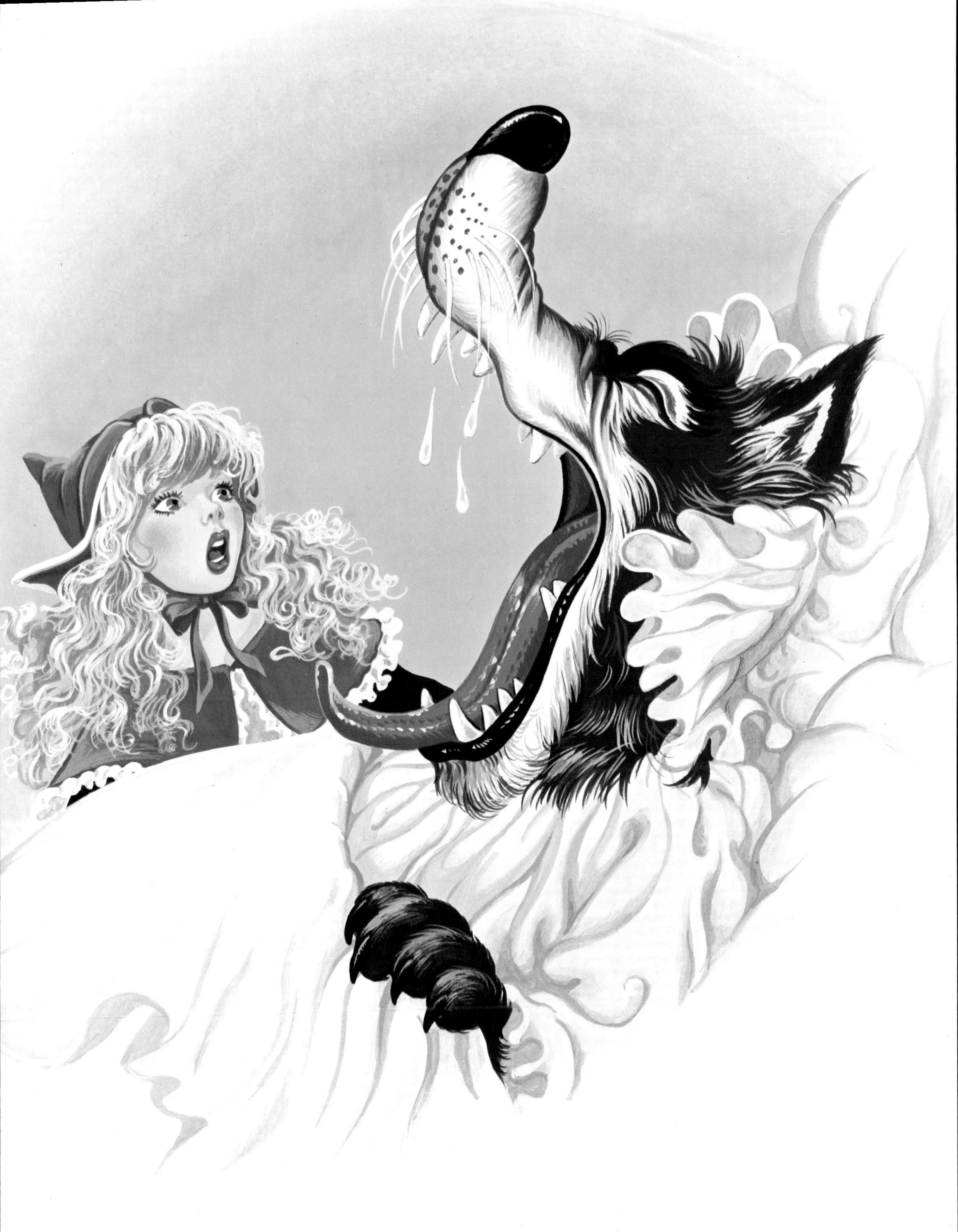

A hunter walking nearby in the forest heard Little Red Riding Hood's screams. He came running and found the wolf lying in the bed.

Realizing what had happened, he quickly killed the wolf and sliced open the wolf's stomach with his hunting knife. Out popped the grandmother and Little Red Riding Hood, safe and sound!

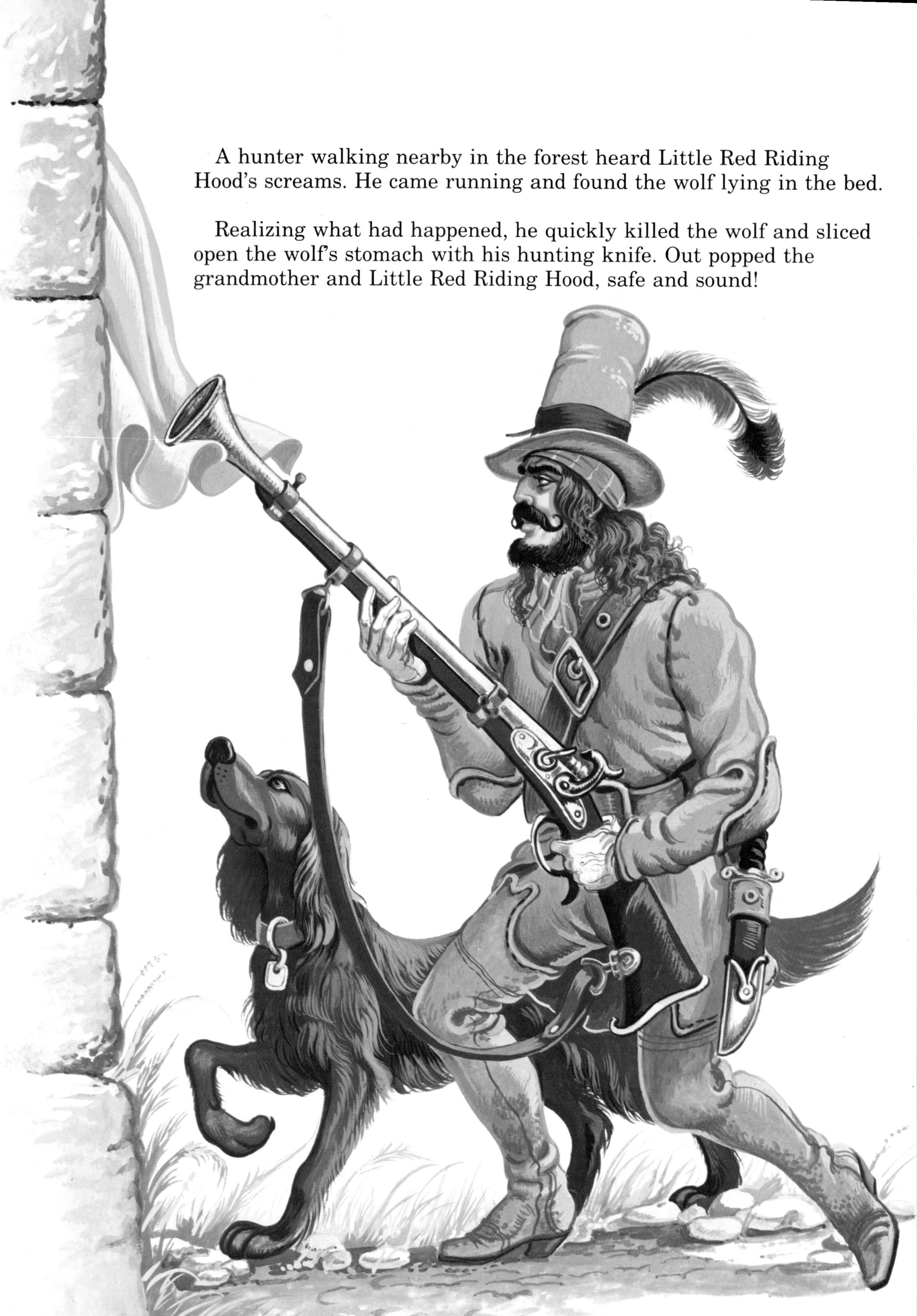